MAX & MADDY
and the Chocolate
Money Mystery

Books by Alexander McCall Smith

Akimbo and the Elephants
Akimbo and the Lions
Akimbo and the Crocodile Man
Akimbo and the Snakes

The Five Lost Aunts of Harriet Bean
Harriet Bean and the League of Cheats
The Cowgirl Aunt of Harriet Bean

Max & Maddy and the Chocolate Money Mystery
Max & Maddy and the Bursting Balloons Mystery

The Perfect Hamburger and Other Delicious Stories

Alexander McCall Smith

MAX & MADDY
and the Chocolate
Money Mystery

Illustrated by Macky Pamintuan

BLOOMSBURY
CHILDREN'S
BOOKS

For Carolyn and Eric

Text copyright © 1997 by Alexander McCall Smith
Illustrations copyright © 2007 by Macky Pamintuan
First published in the U.K. in 1997 by Scholastic Children's Books, London,
a division of Scholastic Ltd.
Published in 2007 in the United States by Bloomsbury U.S.A. Children's Books
Paperback edition published in 2008

Published by Bloomsbury U.S.A. Children's Books
175 Fifth Avenue, New York, New York 10010
Distributed to the trade by Macmillan

The Library of Congress has cataloged the hardcover edition as follows:
McCall Smith, Alexander.
Max and Maddy and the chocolate money mystery / by Alexander McCall Smith ;
illustrations by Macky Pamintuan. — 1st U.S. ed.
p.   cm.
Summary: Asked by a Swiss banker to investigate a series of bank robberies committed by
dogs, young detectives Max and Maddy Twist travel to Switzerland, where they discover
that the man behind the robberies is none other than Professor Sardine.
ISBN-13: 978-1-59990-036-0 • ISBN-10: 1-59990-036-X (hardcover)
[1. Bank robberies—Fiction. 2. Saint Bernard dog—Fiction. 3. Dogs—Fiction.
4. Brothers and sisters—Fiction. 5. Switzerland—Fiction. 6. Mystery and
detective stories.] I. Pamintuan, Macky, ill. II. Title.
PZ7.M47833755May 2007   [Fic]—dc22   2006015569

ISBN-13: 978-1-59990-216-6 • ISBN-10: 1-59990-216-8 (paperback)

Typeset by Westchester Book Composition
Printed in the U.S.A. by Worzalla
2 4 6 8 10 9 7 5 3 1

Contents

Max and Maddy–
Private Detectives

On the very edge of the town where Max and Maddy Twist lived, there was an ice-cream parlor. It was not a large ice-cream parlor—in fact it was pretty small—but it was very popular with people who liked really good ice cream in lots of different flavors (there were thirty-seven, to be exact).

Behind the parlor there was a house, and this is where Max and Maddy lived with their parents. Mr. and Mrs. Twist had not been making ice cream for long. They used to be private detectives and had been the owners of the best private detective agency in the country. They had even won prizes for their detective work—the *Best Disguise Award* (which they won two years running) and the *Most Difficult Clue Solved Award*. Then, without any warning, something terrible happened, and they had been forced out of business.

What happened was not their fault, but the work of an extremely cunning man named Professor Claude Sardine. This man had been wicked since birth. When he was a baby, he had hidden other babies' rattles and made them cry. Then, when he was a little bit older and was at school, he had cheated in the egg-and-spoon relay race, secretly sticking the egg to his spoon so that it would not fall off. A little later, he had soaked all the school chalk in water, so that it would not write when the teacher tried to use it. And then, when he was much bigger—about eighteen—he had ruined the world's most famous bicycle race, the *Tour de France*, by scattering thumbtacks on the roads at night. That was a particularly mean and nasty thing to do, but then Professor Sardine was a very nasty man.

Mr. and Mrs. Twist had once managed to thwart one of Professor Sardine's evil schemes, and he had never forgiven them for it. The professor had gotten ahold of two thousand pairs of underwear and had treated them all with . . . itching powder! He was at the point of selling them at bargain prices to the public when Mr. and Mrs. Twist stepped in and put a stop to it.

They had just been investigating the strange loss of two thousand pairs of underwear from a factory on the edge of town. The only lead they had was a sardine, left at the scene of the crime.

For a while, Mr. and Mrs. Twist were stumped. But not for long. Because soon after that there was another burglary—this time at a joke store. Two thousand bags of itching powder had been stolen, and once again a mysterious sardine was left behind. But here the professor had made his fatal mistake. Little did he know that he was dealing with two real professionals.

The Twists, with the sardines as evidence,

questioned the town's fish seller, deducing—
correctly—that anyone dastardly enough to
steal two thousand pairs of underwear and
two thousand bags of itching powder would
never pay honest money for a couple of sardines. And sure enough, the fish seller was
able to give a very good description of a man
who had entered his shop, stolen the sardines, and run off, laughing in a chilling
manner.

A picture of the professor was soon drawn
up by the Twists and pasted all over town
with the words DO NOT BUY UNDERWEAR
FROM THIS MAN written underneath it. This
spoiled Professor Sardine's fun, and he swore
to drive the Twists out of business.

His revenge had come in the shape of a
simple but very wicked plan. He had gone to
every newspaper in the country and paid for
the publication of a large notice. This notice
simply said that Mr. and Mrs. Twist, the
famous detectives, had been arrested and
sent to prison for thirty-three years and three
months! Of course this was not true, but

everybody believed it, and Mr. and Mrs. Twist's business was ruined. There was nothing for them to do but give up being detectives and open an ice-cream parlor.

Listening to their parents' stories, Max and Maddy soon found out a great deal about how to be private detectives. They also learned a lot from the books that lined the walls of their parents' study. There was a very interesting book called *Two Hundred Simple Disguises*. This book itself could be disguised! If you turned it upside down, it looked exactly like a cheese sandwich, and if you laid it on its side, it looked like an old hairbrush! But their favorite one of all was called *How to Follow People Without Being Seen—Ever*. This book had been written by Mr. and Mrs. Twist themselves, and there was a large photograph of them on the back cover just to prove it.

In their spare time, when they were not reading books about private detection, the two children liked to play a game called Clue. This was great fun, as it involved trying to

find out who had committed a crime just by asking questions and writing down the answers. Max and Maddy were so good at it that they won every time they played with other people. And when the local newspaper announced that there would be a grand Clue competition to find the champion player of the year, it was no surprise that Max and Maddy both entered.

It was not all that easy. They found themselves up against very stiff competition, but at last, after a grand finale filled with nailbiting suspense, the judges announced that the first prize had been won jointly by the two of them.

Mr. and Mrs. Twist were extremely proud.

"This proves it!" crowed Mrs. Twist. "Detective talent runs in our blood. I've always said that!"

It was wonderful to have won the competition, but what happened next was even more exciting. Just a few days later, when the mailman brought the mail, there was a letter for them with an unusual stamp on it.

"Look," said their mother, handing Maddy the letter. "A letter from Switzerland. Do you know anybody there?"

Maddy shook her head and started to open the letter. As she read it through, her jaw dropped with surprise.

"What does it say?" asked Max in a very excited voice. "Read it out loud. It's addressed to me, too."

Maddy read the letter, and now it was Max's turn to be astonished. For the letter from Switzerland was a very exciting one indeed. The person who wrote it, Mr. Conrad Huffendorf, a well-known and very rich Swiss banker, had read about their success in the Clue competition and asked them whether they could possibly solve a mystery for him.

"If you can play Clue so well," he wrote, "then I'm sure you'll be able to solve a mystery for us here in Switzerland. I am a banker, as you may know, and I am very worried about what has been happening. There have been some very large bank robberies, and the police just cannot seem to solve the crimes. Do you think you could help? After all, you're terribly good at Clue."

Max and Maddy looked at their mother.

"Do you think we could?" they asked. "Poor Mr. Huffendorf sounds very worried."

Mrs. Twist thought for a moment. Most parents would say no, of course, but then most parents don't run ice-cream parlors with thirty-seven flavors.

So Mrs. Twist said, "Yes, of course you can go."

She had been a private detective, you see, and she knew that you could never turn down a real mystery. Never.

Suddenly, Maddy noticed a tiny P.S. on the letter, and she read it out loud carefully. This is what it said:

"P.S. Of course we'll reward you handsomely for your help. We can either pay in money (we've still got a little bit left) or, if you prefer, in bars of chocolate. Switzerland, as you know, makes the best chocolate in the world. So you just decide. Money or chocolate, but not both!"

Which would you have chosen, I wonder?
Really! Is that your answer? Well, well!
And which do you think Max and Maddy
chose? Read on, please. You'll find out later.

Wanted for
Bank Robbery!

Welcome to Switzerland!" said Mr. Huf-fendorf, taking off his hat and giving a small bow.

Max and Maddy, fresh from their journey by plane and train, saw a small, rather round man standing in front of them. He was wearing a black coat with a velvet collar and tiny pebblelike spectacles. He was very polite and insisted on carrying their suitcases for them. And when they were sitting in his car, which was waiting outside, he put a thick blanket over their knees, just to make sure that they were warm enough.

As they sped along the streets on the way

to Mr. Huffendorf's house, they saw snow everywhere—on the roofs of the houses, on the branches of the trees, and even on people's hats. And behind the town, climbing up toward the sky, there were mountains, and these too were covered with snow, like white icing on a cake.

Mr. Huffendorf said nothing for a while, but then he suddenly turned to Max and asked him a question.

"Where do you keep your money?" he inquired, peering at Max through his tiny round spectacles.

"I don't have very much," said Max, thinking of how he had spent his savings, every last cent of it, on two large bars of chocolate to eat on the journey.

"But you must get allowance money," said Mr. Huffendorf. "Where do you put that?"

"In my pocket, I suppose," answered Max. "Or, if I decide to save it up, I put it in my pencil case, or maybe in the drawer where I keep my socks."

Mr. Huffendorf shook his head sadly. "Oh,

dear!" he said. "Oh, dear! Oh, dear! The best place for allowance money is a Swiss bank! Everybody knows that. Now, if you gave me your allowance money, I would put it in my bank, and then it would be as safe as can be, all tucked away in the Huffendorf Bank!"

Max thought for a moment. "But what about these bank robberies?" he asked. "No robber would think to look in my sock drawer . . ."

Mr. Huffendorf suddenly looked taken aback. "I suppose I'd forgotten about that," he said sadly. "You're quite right. Swiss banks aren't as safe as they used to be, I'm sorry to say. And all because of these dreadful robberies."

The banker paused and looked at the children.

"I have a photograph of one of the robbers, you know. Would you like to see it?"

"Well," said Maddy, "if we're going to help you find the robbers, I think we should know what they look like."

Mr. Huffendorf fished into the inner

pocket of his jacket and took out a small folded poster. On the bottom, printed in very large letters, it said: WANTED.

"Here," he said. "This is one of them. It was taken by a secret camera in the bank at the very moment of the robbery."

He handed the poster over to the children, who studied it carefully. Then they looked at each other in confusion.

"But it's a dog!" said Max. "You said it was a photograph of a bank robber."

Mr. Huffendorf smiled. "Exactly," he said. "It's a photograph of one of our famous Swiss mountain dogs, a Saint Bernard. They are usually used to rescue people who have gotten lost in the snow. They have wonderful noses, you see. But now, I'm ashamed to say, they seem to have taken up bank robbery. Every single one of these robberies has been carried out by a dog!"

As the car made its way along the winding mountain roads that led to Mr. Huffendorf's house, the two children listened

in astonishment to the story of the extraordinary robberies.

"The first time it happened," said Mr. Huffendorf, "people could hardly believe it. The dog came into the bank, jumped over the counter, and immediately started to collect piles of cash in its mouth. Saint Bernards have very large mouths, you know, and he managed to fit an awful lot in. Then he growled—he couldn't bark, because his mouth was full—and he ran out the door. Everybody was too astonished to chase him, and it was all over in minutes."

That was the first bank robbery, explained Mr. Huffendorf. The next one, which took place a few weeks later, was much the same, although this time it was a different dog. At this bank, the dog slipped in unseen and then managed to run up to the manager's desk and start growling at him in a most unfriendly way. By growling and barking, the dog had pushed the manager back toward the safe, and it threatened to bite him until the man had opened the safe door. Then the dog had bolted inside, grabbed a large bag of gold coins in its jaws, and dashed out again.

Several more banks had been robbed in exactly the same way, and the dogs, which were different ones on each occasion, got away with it every time. Somebody had tried once to chase one, but the dog had been too cunning. It is easy for a dog to get away from a human being, as it can squeeze through spaces that humans cannot get through. It's not all that easy for a person to crawl under a car and emerge on the other side in no more than a second or two. Nor are people very good at wiggling through smelly storm drains full of mud and old leaves. But dogs love that, and so it was easy for them to get away.

Mr. Huffendorf finished telling his story and then looked hopefully at Max and Maddy.

"Please do something about this," he said. "We really need your help."

Later that day, while Mr. Huffendorf went to attend to some business, the two children stood in front of the great window of his living room, looking out at the snow-covered valley below.

"This is a very strange story," said Max. "I've never heard of anything like it. Dogs that rob banks!"

"I can't see how we can help," said Maddy. "If the police can't find these dogs, then how are we going to do any better?"

Max was silent. He was staring out the window, and Maddy knew that when he did that, he was thinking very hard.

"I think I've got an idea," he said after a while. "I think I know what to do. Tell me, Maddy, why do you think these dogs are robbing banks?"

Maddy scratched her head. "Because they're bad?" she suggested. "Because they're bad dogs?"

Max shook his head. "No," he said. "Bad dogs chase cars and cats. They don't rob banks. The only reason why a dog would rob a bank is because it's been taught to do it. Somebody has trained these dogs to do their dirty work. Somebody has decided that the safest way to steal money from the bank is to get a dog to do it! As long as the dog can slip away, you're never going to get caught. Nobody will see you, nobody will know who you are. You just wait around the corner and take the money from the dog's mouth. Then you stuff the dog into a van and off you go."

Maddy thought for a moment. It sounded very strange, but it must be true. So what were they going to do about it?

Max looked at his sister and smiled. "I've got a plan," he said. "I'll tell you about it later. The first thing we have to do is to get a Saint Bernard dog for ourselves. Then we'll put an advertisement in the newspaper!"

Maddy felt puzzled, but she knew that her brother's plans were usually very good ones, and she was sure that this would be a good one too. But what could he possibly want with a St. Bernard dog? She was soon to find out.

St. Bernard Dog
Seeks Home

A Saint Bernard dog?" exclaimed Mr. Huffendorf. "*You* want *me* to get you a Saint Bernard dog?"

"Yes, please," said Max. "And we'd like a very obedient one, if possible."

Mr. Huffendorf scratched his head. "Well, I suppose I can do that," he said. "I think my brother knows a man who has a cousin whose friend's aunt breeds these dogs. Should I ask him to ask him to ask her to ask him to ask her?"

It was agreed that Mr. Huffendorf would try as soon as possible to borrow a dog and bring it to the house. He went off to do this, while Max and Maddy went out into the garden, which was deep in snow, to throw snowballs and build a large snow dog.

A few hours later, they saw Mr. Huffendorf's car winding back up the road to the house. The driver was in the front, and in the backseat sat Mr. Huffendorf and the largest dog the children had ever seen. The car stopped outside the front door and Mr. Huffendorf got out, followed by the dog. The dog looked around, sniffed at the air, and gave an enthusiastic bark. Then it followed Mr. Huffendorf into the house to be introduced to Max and Maddy.

"This is Rudolf," said Mr. Huffendorf, and as he spoke, the dog held out a paw to be shaken.

It was a splendid dog, and like all Swiss dogs, it was extremely obedient and well mannered. It sat politely on the floor, and it stood up when asked. When you called out, "Come here!" it trotted over to sit at your side, and when you said, "Lie down!" it lay down exactly where it was standing at the time, no questions asked.

After they had spent a while getting to know Rudolf, Mr. Huffendorf asked Max to explain his plan.

"It's quite simple," said Max. "One of the best rules for being a good private detective is this: *It's much easier to get the crooks to come to you than for you to go to them!* So, if we put an advertisement in the newspapers saying that the best-trained Saint Bernard dog in Switzerland is looking for a home, that might be very interesting to the bank robbers. After all, their robberies are going so well that they'll be needing more dogs to help them."

Mr. Huffendorf looked doubtful. "Perhaps," he said, and then, "Well, we can at least try. But remember that we have to give Rudolf back. His owner is very fond of him. He won't come to any harm, will he?"

"I hope not," said Max.

At this, Rudolf gave a loud bark, as if he understood everything that had been said. He was clearly a very intelligent dog, and it was just possible that he had picked up some of the plan. Dogs, after all, understand much more than they would like us to believe, and Rudolf perhaps had heard and taken in the word "robbers." Yes, he thought. Robbers! You've picked just the right dog to help you! Oh, yes! *Grrr*! Just let me at them!

The advertisement appeared in the newspaper the next day.

EXCELLENT ST. BERNARD DOG SEEKS HOME

Rudolf, our beloved St. Bernard, is a hardworking dog who is also very obedient. But St. Bernards are very big, and we are moving to a very small house. So could some kind person please look after him?

Tel: 6283

There were one or two telephone calls that morning. One of them was from a lady who wanted Rudolf to pull a dog cart for her. Another was from a man who wanted him to scare cats out of his yard. Neither of these sounded like a bank robber, though, and Mr. Huffendorf thanked them politely and said that he would have to think about it. Then the doorbell rang, and this time it was a rather suspicious-looking man.

"Where's the dog?" he said rudely. "I'd like to see him."

Mr. Huffendorf invited him in while Max and Maddy went to fetch Rudolf.

"Rather a scruffy-looking dog," said the man with a sneer. "I've seen much better."

Max shot Maddy a glance. As detectives they could tell that this was the man. When you looked at him, his eyes slid away and his nose twitched ever so slightly. That was always a sign.

"He's a very obedient dog," said Maddy. "Look, if I tell him to lie down, he'll do so immediately."

The man watched as Rudolf went through his paces.

"I suppose I can take him," he said at the end of it all. "Over here, dog. You're coming with me."

Rudolf seemed unwilling to go with his new owner, but with a little encouragement from Max, he eventually allowed the man to fit a leash onto his collar and drag him out the door.

The man walked down the road with a miserable-looking Rudolf walking beside him, glancing backward from time to time to see if his new friends were coming with him. They were, of course, but they remembered everything they had read in their parents' book *How to Follow People Without Being Seen—Ever,* and Rudolf would never have noticed them. When he looked behind him, as he did from time to time, did he think that there was something odd about that bush on the edge of the road— the one with the branches that seemed to be moving ever so slightly? Of course he did not. And when he saw that very tall person with a long coat and a hat pulled down over his eyes,

did he think that it was really a girl perched on a boy's shoulders? Not for a moment.

There was a small train station at the end of the road, and it was here that the man went, pulling Rudolf behind him. Max and Maddy waited, crouching behind a snowdrift at the edge of the railway line. When the train came, they would be able to slip into one of the carriages without being seen by the man or Rudolf.

"I hope we don't lose Rudolf," whispered Maddy. "We promised to bring him back."

"Don't worry," said Max. "We won't lose him."

When the train came, the two children were ready. While the man mounted the steps with Rudolf, they quickly shot into the next carriage and were safely seated by the time the conductor blew his whistle. Then they were off, with the little Swiss train pulling bravely up the line as it wound its way farther into the mountains.

At the first stop, they watched carefully out of their window to see if the man got off.

He did not. Nor did he get off at the next stop. But at the one after that, they saw the carriage door open and the man step out, closely followed by Rudolf.

Max and Maddy slipped off the train and took shelter behind a newspaper stand. Then, making sure to keep their distance, they followed the man down the street, sidling into doorways whenever it looked as if he might stop or turn around.

A cable car left from the end of the village. Supported on towering metal posts, the cable ran up the side of the mountain and disappeared into the clouds. It was mainly for skiers, but it was also very useful for people who lived in the houses that dotted the higher slopes.

Max and Maddy watched as the man put Rudolf into a cable car and then climbed in himself. They waited for a while, until they were sure they would not be seen; then they quickly bought a ticket and took the next car that came along. Max did not like heights— they made him feel dizzy—so he closed his eyes as the car swung away from the cable station. Maddy was fine. She liked looking down at the tops of the pine trees beneath them and at the great banks of snow.

"Oh, look!" she shouted. "Skiers down below us!"

"I can't look," said Max miserably. "Oh, Maddy, when are we going to get there?"

Maddy looked ahead. There was still a long way to go and the ground was even farther away below them.

"A pretty long way," she said, thinking, I wonder what would happen if the cable broke? Would the snow break our fall?

Max was thinking exactly the same thing, and the thought made him turn a little bit green. He was also thinking about how they would have to come down again, which would probably be even worse.

"If only we hadn't come to Switzerland in the first place," he said under his breath. "If only we'd gone somewhere flat, with no mountains—like Holland, or Texas, or somewhere like that!"

It's Professor Sardine!

At long last, they reached the top of the cable. Maddy pushed back the door and Max opened his eyes, slowly at first, just to make sure that they were no longer halfway up the mountain.

There was no sign of the man at first, but after a few moments, they saw him walking off in the direction of a group of trees in the snow. Rudolf was plodding along beside him. Like all St. Bernard dogs, he felt at home in the snow, and had large padded feet to stop him from sinking in.

They waited until the man was out of sight before they set off. It was easy to find his tracks in the snow and follow him through the wood and into a ravine that ran down the mountainside.

"There it is," said Maddy, pointing to a small group of buildings in the distance. "That's where he's going."

Max looked in the direction that his sister was pointing. It seemed to be a small farm, with a house, a barn, and one or two sheds, all perched on the mountainside.

"We'll have to be careful," said Max. "If we climb up a little, we could get into those trees just behind the house and have a look at the place from there."

Maddy thought this was a good idea, and they quickly made their way across the mountainside to the shelter of the trees. Then, creeping forward in the snow, they peered down at the buildings beneath them. And at that exact moment, two things happened, one after the other, that made them realize they had been right all along.

The first thing was that there was suddenly a loud barking from one of the sheds. This was interesting, as it was not just one dog that was barking, but four or five, and they were all deep barks, exactly like the barks made by a St. Bernard dog.

But the second thing was even more important. As the dogs started to bark, a man came out of the back door of the farmhouse. It was not the man who had brought Rudolf, but somebody very different. He was looking down at the ground first, but then he suddenly looked up, and for a moment Max and Maddy got a good view of his face. It was not a face they had ever seen before—in the flesh, at least—but it was still a face they knew very well from a photograph that their father had showed them. It was none other than Professor Claude Sardine!

The children stayed absolutely still, hardly daring to breathe in case the white clouds of their breath should give them away. But Professor Sardine had not seen them, and he went over to the shed where the dogs were barking. He opened the door, and five dogs rushed out, cavorting in the snow, all eager

for some exercise. Professor Sardine reached down to pat one of them and then apparently changed his mind—and gave it a sharp kick!

"Did you see that?" whispered Maddy indignantly.

"Typical of him!" her brother replied under his breath. "That's just the sort of man he is."

The two detectives watched while Professor Sardine exercised the dogs.

He did this in a very unkind way. He tied a large bone to a string, and he then threw the bone into the snow. The dogs raced after it, hoping to have a chew on the delicious morsel, but it was always snatched away from them before they reached it. Then Professor Sardine would throw it in the opposite direction and laugh cruelly when the poor dogs were tricked again. After a while, though, he tired of all this, and he shut the dogs back in the shed. Then he returned to the farmhouse, slamming the door behind him.

"So it's Professor Sardine who's behind the robberies," said Max quietly. "We should have known!"

"Yes," agreed Maddy. "And this is such a good place for his headquarters, high up on the mountain where there's nobody to get suspicious."

Max thought for a moment. "We could go right back and tell Mr. Huffendorf," he said. "Or we could try to figure things out ourselves."

Maddy shivered, not from cold but from fear. Max always wanted to figure things out himself, and sometimes she thought it was a little bit safer to let other people do that.

"What could we do?" she asked.

Max smiled. A plan was forming in his mind, and it seemed to him that it would be a lot of fun—as long as it went well. If it didn't go well, though . . . perhaps it was best not to think about that.

"Let's try to find the money," he said. "Then we'll free the dogs and take them with us. That way, we'll rescue the dogs, get Mr. Huffendorf's money back for him, and stop Professor Sardine right in his tracks!"

Maddy's mouth dropped open. It sounded

so simple, the way Max had put it, but it would be very dangerous. What if they were caught? What would Professor Sardine do with them? It was bound to be something terrible. Perhaps he would push them down a glacier or something like that.

Max, though, seemed to have his mind made up.

"Now listen, Maddy," he whispered. "Here's the plan."

She listened with her heart in her mouth. It was very dangerous indeed, and she was convinced that it would fail.

Max's plan was simple—or so he thought. He would creep down to the farmhouse and make his way to the side. There was a pile of firewood there, and he could crouch behind it. In the meantime, Maddy would very quietly make her way down to the back of the dog shed. Then, on a signal from Max (a quick whistle) she would start to scratch at the wooden wall of the dog shed, while hiding behind it. This would disturb the dogs, who would bark. Professor Sardine or his assistant would then come out of the back door to see what was disturbing the dogs. Of course, Maddy would stop scratching the wood and the dogs would no longer bark, but by that time the back door of the house would be open and Max could dash into the farmhouse without being seen.

"And then?" said Maddy. "What then?"

"Once I'm in the house, I'll have a good look around," he said. "If I find the money— and I'm sure I will—I'll get it out somehow. Then we'll release the dogs and get back to the cable station as quickly as we can. That's all."

Maddy stared at her brother. Had he gone crazy? (Boys sometimes did.) Did he really think that such an elaborate scheme would work? With a sinking heart, she realized that he did, and she knew that once her brother had decided on a plan, nothing would stop him. So she nodded and said that she would try.

"Good," whispered Max, patting her on the arm. "Best of luck! Here goes!"

The Trapdoor
under the Bed

Maddy waited until Max was hidden behind the woodpile. Then she drew a deep breath and ran as fast as she could to the back of the dog shed. So far so good, she thought. Now all she had to do was to wait for Max's signal.

This came a minute or so later, a low whistle that anybody else would have thought was a bird call but that she knew was her brother. At this, Maddy took out the twig she had tucked into her pocket and began to scratch at the back of the shed.

For a dog it was an interesting noise, and it meant only one thing—rats! Immediately after Maddy started, the dogs began to whine and bark, and the more she scratched, the harder the dogs barked. What a rat it must be, thought the St. Bernards. Oh, quick! Let us at it! We'll teach it a thing or two!

Exactly as Max had hoped, the back door was flung open, and Professor Sardine strode out.

"Why are you making that noise?" he yelled angrily. "You wretched dogs! I'll teach you to disturb my afternoon nap!"

The irate professor marched to the dog shed and banged loudly on the door. He and his assistant had spent the entire night out, planning the next robbery, and they were now extremely tired. The one thing he wanted to do was sleep so he would be wide awake for the wicked schemes they had planned for that night.

As the professor reached the shed, Max rose to his feet, checked that the coast was clear, and ran around the side of the house. The back door was open, and he shot in while Professor Sardine was still threatening and shouting at the dogs.

Inside, Max found himself in a kitchen, with a large wood-burning stove, a table, and onions and hams hanging from the ceiling. He did not stay there, though, but quickly opened a door into a hallway. Several doors led off this, and Max took the first, hoping that he would discover nobody in the room behind it. But he was wrong. There *was* somebody in the room. It was the man who had come for Rudolf, and he was lying on a bed in a corner . . . fast asleep!

Max caught his breath and closed the door silently behind him. If you've ever been in a room with a sleeping person whom you don't want to wake, you know what it's like. People are never totally still when they're asleep. They snuffle and move their toes. And at any moment, you think the slightest movement from you will wake them up.

Max looked around him. There was another bed in the room with a crumpled comforter, but not much else. There was a wardrobe, a small chest of drawers, and a table on which some papers lay scattered.

Max crept over to the table and picked up one of the papers. There were columns of numbers that had been added up and ticked with a pencil. It was as if somebody had been adding up sums of money.

Sums of money! Max's heart gave a leap. If somebody had been adding up money, then the money could be hidden here, right in this room. Very quietly, he moved over toward the wardrobe and opened the door. There was nothing. He moved to the chest of drawers and slid open the top drawer. It was full of socks and handkerchiefs. He looked in the second drawer, and that was full of shirts. The third drawer was empty.

Max felt very disappointed. He would have to search the rest of the house now, and that would take time. It would also be dangerous, as at any moment he could bump into Professor Sardine. Yet he would have to do it.

There was a noise, making Max start— Professor Sardine was back in the house! Max thought for a moment, his glance falling on the crumpled comforter on the bed. With a

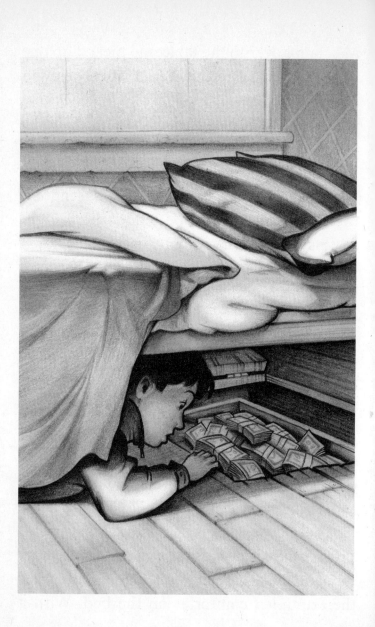

sudden feeling of shock, he realized that the reason why the comforter was crumpled was that somebody had been sleeping in the bed, and that person could only be Professor Sardine himself.

Max would have to hide before Professor Sardine came back. He thought of the wardrobe, but he was worried that the door might not stay closed. So that left only one place—under Professor Sardine's bed.

Professor Sardine came back into the room, muttering to himself.

"Those dogs," he said. "They bark and bark for no reason. I'll have to get a whip. That'll teach them."

He sat down on the bed, took off his shoes, and flung them down on the floor. Although he was making a lot of noise, the man on the other bed slept soundly.

"Humph!" snorted Professor Sardine. "It's fine for you. I'm the one who has to do all the thinking around here. I'm the one who needs the sleep!"

Underneath Professor Sardine's bed, Max felt the mattress sag toward him as the professor slumped down in bed. Fortunately, though, there was still enough room, and Max was able to move his arms and legs. He turned slightly in order to be more comfortable, and it was then that he saw it. There was a trapdoor, directly under the bed! If this was the room they counted the money in, thought Max, then where better to keep the money itself? With a sudden sense of excitement, Max realized that he was probably lying directly above large amounts of money, and that all he would have to do would be to wait for Professor Sardine to go to sleep. Then he could pry open the trapdoor and see what lay beneath. He was sure it would be money. Lots of money. Lots and *lots* of money.

Professor Sardine tossed and turned on the bed above Max's head. Then at last, he was still, and Max heard a regular, snoring sound coming from above him. This was his chance, and as carefully as he could, he began to open the trapdoor, trying to avoid making the slightest sound.

It was a difficult task, but at last the trapdoor lay open, and Max was able to peer down into the space below. For a few moments, he could see nothing in the dark, but then he slowly began to make it out. He had been right—exactly right. Immediately below him was a large, open box with rope handles at each end. And inside the box, neatly stacked, was a pile of cash. He had found Mr. Huffendorf's money!

Being as quiet as he possibly could, Max reached down through the trapdoor and took ahold of the crate's handles. Max did his very best, but even so from time to time he bumped a shoulder or an elbow against the sagging mattress directly above him, and at one point even made Professor Sardine stir. After a few minutes of trying, he realized that it was simply not possible to get the crate out without moving the bed. Max sighed—he was so close to rescuing the money, but now he would simply have to give up. Or . . . he stopped. He had just seen that the bed, like many old-fashioned beds, had little wheels to make it easier to move around the room.

Max wiggled out from under the bed and very gently took ahold of the headboard. Then he pushed it lightly, just to see, and the bed moved! Slowly he began to push it across the floor, away from the trapdoor. Professor Sardine slept on, completely unaware of what was happening. He'll get a surprise when he wakes up, thought Max.

Max turned around to look at the trapdoor, and in that instant he let go of the headboard. If the bedroom floor had been normal, then there would have been no problem. But the floor was not normal—it slanted badly, and before Max could do anything about it, the bed began to move on its own.

His heart in his throat, Max ran after the bed, which had now crossed most of the bedroom floor. For a moment or two he thought that it would collide with the door, but it did not, and instead it shot through into the hallway. From there it gathered speed, pursued by Max, until it slid smoothly and gently into a large closet and came to a halt.

Max crept up to the bed and peered at Professor Sardine. His peculiar journey had not woken him, and he was still fast asleep. Max tiptoed out of the closet and closed the door. There was a key in the lock, and with a smile, he locked the door behind him. That took care of Professor Sardine! The professor would probably be able to break the door down, or shout for his assistant to free him, but that would take some time.

Now came the difficult part. The crate was far too heavy for one person to lift, and Max had no choice but to drag it. This was difficult to do without making a noise, and Max was sure that at any moment he would wake the sleeping assistant. But somehow he did not, and he soon found himself dragging the crate along the hallway and into the kitchen. From there it was easy to open the back door and push the heavy crate down the steps and onto the snow.

Maddy had been watching. When she saw the back door open, her heart stood still. But she breathed a sigh of relief when she saw that it was her brother—with a large crate. Was that the money? she wondered. It must be!

Max straightened up and looked toward their hiding place. Putting his fingers to his mouth, he whistled, and motioned to Maddy to come down.

"You've done it," Maddy said softly, as she reached his side and looked down into the open crate. "You've found the money!"

Max nodded. "Yes," he whispered. "It's all in this crate, but it's very heavy. I can't carry it by myself. You'll have to help me, once we've gotten the dogs out."

They left the crate where it was and ran over to the dog shed. The dogs had heard something, and when Max and Maddy opened the door, the great animals were all over them, licking their faces with affection and wagging their heavy, furry tails. Rudolf was particularly pleased to see them, and he insisted on covering Maddy's face with great, wet, doglike kisses before she managed to push him off of her and calm him down. One of the other dogs opened his mouth, as if he was going to bark, but Rudolf, sensing that it was important for them all to keep quiet, glared at him and growled. That stopped the bark before it even left the dog's throat.

"This way," said Max, calling Rudolf to his side. "Follow me, and tell the other dogs to come too."

Rudolf understood perfectly. He gave a growl and a grunt to the other dogs, and they all fell into line behind him. Then Max and Maddy, with the five St. Bernard dogs in an obedient line behind them, ran back to the crate. Together Max and Maddy picked it up, one person holding each end, and began to make their way as fast as they could through the snow toward the cable station.

It was a long walk, and a hard one too, as much of it was uphill. As they went along, the crate seemed to get heavier and heavier, and Max and Maddy had to stop more and more often to rest and regain their strength. But they made progress, and soon they had crossed the ravine and were able to look back at the farm buildings, now far below them in the brilliant white snow fields.

"Look how far we've come," said Max. "Now all we have to do is . . ."

He stopped. As they looked down toward the farm, they saw the back door burst open and two tiny figures run out. They saw one of the figures spin around and look up toward them, pointing in their direction.

"He got out of the closet," Max said. "He'll be furious!"

"Closet?" asked Maddy. "Who was in what closet?"

"Professor Sardine," said Max. "You see, there were wheels on his bed and the floor was slanted, and there was an open door . . ." He stopped. "I'll tell you all about it later. I think they've seen us!"

Cable Car Adventure

Max and Maddy lost no time. Picking up the crate, they plunged ahead, almost falling over one another in their haste. The snow was deep, and their feet sank down with each step, but they realized that if they did not hurry, they would soon be caught. The professor and his assistant had snow shoes and could make much quicker progress than the children, who were wearing ordinary snow boots.

The dogs realized that something was wrong, and they barked encouragement to the children and defiance toward their pursuers. But it did not do a great deal of good, as the next time they looked behind them, they saw that they were losing ground quickly.

"They'll catch us in no time," moaned Max. "They're much faster than we are."

Now it was Maddy's turn to have a good idea.

"Look," she said. "It's now mostly downhill from here to the cable station. If we had a toboggan, we could go much faster."

"That's not much use," panted Max. "We haven't got a toboggan. You might as well say, 'If we had an airplane . . . '"

He stopped. He saw what Maddy meant now, and it was a wonderful idea.

"The crate!" he exclaimed. "Why don't we use it as a toboggan?"

"That's just what I thought," said Maddy. "But we must hurry. They're getting closer and closer all the time."

They put down the crate and pointed it in the direction of the cable station. Then, with Maddy getting in the front and Max sitting immediately behind her—both of them perched on top of the piles of money—they gave the crate a good push with their arms.

It was slow at first, but after a moment or two it started to slide more quickly. Then, as the ground began to slope more sharply, the crate really picked up speed, and soon it was rushing along the ground like a bobsled in a mountain race. The dogs thought this was tremendous fun, and they galloped along beside the crate, the fresh white powder flying off their feet in tiny snow showers.

When their pursuers saw the children shooting off in their makeshift toboggan, they shouted out in fury and broke into a run. It's not easy to run in snow—in fact, it's impossible—as the two men were soon to find out. Down went Professor Sardine, flat on his face in the snow. His assistant reached down to pick him up, and then he slipped and landed on top of him. Professor Sardine now struggled to his feet and reached down to pull his assistant up, but the assistant tugged hard on his hand and then suddenly

let go, which made Professor Sardine fall over backward and slide away on the snow.

"You idiot!" yelled Professor Sardine at his assistant. "They're getting away! Quick, after them!"

Of course, in their makeshift toboggan the two children reached the cable station well before the two men chasing them. They drew to a halt just as an empty cable car reached the top, and without wasting any time they bundled the dogs inside and then dragged their toboggan crate in behind them.

The cable car began its journey down just as the professor and his assistant reached the top of the hill above the cable station. The professor shouted out and shook his fist, but the children just laughed. There was nothing he could do to them now. Once they reached the bottom, they would immediately telephone Mr. Huffendorf and tell him to come and collect his money. He would telephone the police, and before too long Professor Sardine and his evil assistant would be safely locked up in jail.

Or so the children thought. They had not counted on the fact that they were dealing with one of the most cunning and determined villains in the world, and he still had one or two tricks up his sleeve. In fact, although the children did not realize it, they were just about to find themselves faced with the greatest danger they had ever encountered in their lives.

Halfway down the mountainside, while Max was sitting with his eyes firmly closed so that he could not see the drop, and while Maddy was talking soothingly to the frightened St. Bernard dogs, the cable car suddenly stopped.

"Have we arrived at the bottom?" asked Max, not daring to open his eyes. "That seemed pretty quick."

Maddy looked down. They were nowhere near the bottom, and in fact they were way above the top of a tall pine tree.

"I'm afraid we haven't," she said. "The cable car has just stopped. There's something wrong."

Max gave a groan as he realized what had

happened. Professor Sardine must have done something to stop the cable car, and now he had them at his mercy. All he would have to do was to get a high ladder and climb up to catch them. There would be nothing they could do.

Max was right. Up at the cable station, Professor Sardine and his desperate assistant had overpowered and tied up the man in charge of the controls. Then they had pulled the lever that stopped the great engine from winding up the cable. Now all they had to do was to fetch the ladders that the cable car crew used to fix the cable, drag them down the hill, and climb up to where the children were trapped. It was all perfectly simple, although they hadn't decided exactly what they would do with the children when they caught them. Still, there would be plenty of time to think of that . . .

Maddy saw them coming and grabbed her brother's arm.

"Look," she said. "I know you feel dizzy up here, but look over there."

Max looked up at the mountainside above

them. There were two figures carrying a very long ladder, struggling down through the snow toward them. Max let out a groan.

"It's all over," he said. "We're trapped."

Maddy shook her head. "No," she said. "Don't give up yet. Here, give me your scarf."

Max unwound the long scarf that Mr. Huffendorf had lent him, while Maddy did the same with hers. Then, knotting them together at one end, Maddy began to dangle the scarf out of the open window of the cable car. When it was hanging out as far as it would go, she tied the end of the newly made scarf-rope to the handle of the door.

Next, sticking her head out of the window, Maddy looked down. The scarf was blowing a bit in the wind, but she could see that it just reached the top of the tree below them. That was what she had hoped for, and she gave a great sigh of relief.

"We're going to be all right, Max," she said calmly. "All you have to do now is climb down the scarf and grab ahold of the top branches of the pine tree. Then let go of the scarf."

Max gulped. "And then?" he said.

"Pine trees are very thin and bendy," said Maddy calmly. "The tree will bend down like a spring and lower you gently to the ground. That's how it should work." She paused. "Should I go first?"

Max nodded. "Please," he said. "I promise I'll come after you. I promise."

Maddy now turned to the crate and took off her coat. Slipping the coat over the crate, she tied the arms firmly, making a very secure bag.

"This will stop the money from falling out," she said. "Now all we have to do is to throw it down into the snow."

Together they pushed the crate to the open door of the cable car and gave it a shove. Down it went, turning over and over as it fell, until it reached the snow and dropped in with a satisfying plop.

Now it was Maddy's turn, and she bravely let herself down on the scarf until she was in a position to grab for the tree. Once she had done that, the cable car gave a lurch as it was lightened, and Max's stomach seemed to turn upside down within him.

For Maddy it was an even worse feeling. As she grabbed the tree, she felt it give beneath her, and it seemed that she would plummet to the ground. But the branches held, and just before her feet touched the snow, her fall was broken. She let go of the tree just at the right time and found herself firmly on her feet, exactly next to the spot where the crate had fallen.

"Your turn now, Max," she called up at the swaying cable car. "Hurry up!"

Gingerly, Max let himself down the scarf, trying as hard as he could not to look below him. Then he grabbed the tree and down he went as the trunk bent under his weight.

"Let go!" shouted Maddy as Max's feet neared the ground. "Let go now!"

Max may have heard her, or he may not. Whatever the reason, he did not let go of the tree, and so the trunk bent back up again like a spring that has just been released. Then Max let go, but at entirely the wrong time.

As he let go, it was as if Max had been shot from a giant catapult. Head over heels he went, the wind rushing through his hair, the ground getting farther and farther away beneath him. Then he started to drop down, down, like a stone, and he disappeared with a puff of white into a great snow bank.

"Max!" shouted Maddy in despair. "Max, are you all right?"

Up above in the cable car, Rudolf had seen all this. Now, deep inside him, his St. Bernard nature reminded him of his duty. This is exactly what St. Bernard dogs have been bred to do. Their task is to dig people out from the snow, and a tiny voice inside Rudolf told him that his grandfather, and his great-grandfather, and even his great-great-grandfather were watching him, waiting for him to do what was expected of him.

With a huge leap, Rudolf launched himself into space. Down he went, to be followed, one after another, by all the other St. Bernard dogs. To Maddy, standing below, her mouth wide open with astonishment, the dogs looked like a squadron of airplanes, their feet spread wide, their great ears blowing behind them in the wind.

The dogs fell down when they landed in the snow, but not one of them stayed down. Up they went, shaking the snow from their coats, and rushed over to the place where Max had disappeared. Then, howling with excitement, they burrowed and dug, hurling the snow in every direction like snow plows gone wild.

Poor Max! It was bad enough being buried in the snow, but to find himself suddenly being licked by five large pink tongues was almost too much. So he struggled out from the hole and ran back to where Maddy was waiting for him.

"You're safe!" she cried, giving her brother a welcoming hug.

Max cast an anxious glance up the mountainside. "Yes," he said. "Thanks to Rudolf and his friends. But we haven't got a moment to lose. The professor will be down here any minute now. We've got to get going."

Chocolate Money!

They began to drag the crate down the mountainside, but it was very difficult, and they soon realized that they would never manage to get away if they took it with them.

"We'll have to leave it," said Maddy. "The important thing is for us to escape."

Max thought for a moment. He looked at the dogs, who were waiting patiently for their next order. Then he looked at Maddy and smiled.

"We'll bury it," he said. "We'll get Rudolf and his team to dig a hole and then they'll fill it in. Professor Sardine will think we've still got the crate and he'll chase after us rather than look for the money."

Maddy agreed that this was an excellent idea, and they quickly organized the dogs into digging a deep hole at the foot of a tree. Then, when the crate had been safely dropped into it, the dogs very quickly closed the hole again, leaving no traces at all. Maddy carefully marked a tiny cross on the tree with her penknife—so they'd know where to find it again.

In the meantime, Professor Sardine and his assistant had been struggling down the hill toward them, and Max and Maddy had a nasty surprise when they looked up and saw the two men getting closer by the minute. The professor and his assistant had not seen the hole being dug, but the children knew that if they were caught, the professor would soon be able to force them to tell where the crate was hidden.

"We'll never get away," gasped Maddy. "They're much too close."

Max looked up at the two approaching

figures. So did Rudolf, and he frowned—a great St. Bernard frown that knit his brows into a hundred furrows. Then he growled, and at his growl, all the other dogs swung their heads around and looked in the direction of the two men.

Max and Maddy watched in amazement as the dogs formed themselves into a long line and began to bark fiercely.

"They're giving us the chance to get away," said Max. "Quick, let's get down the hill!"

The sight of the snarling dogs stopped Professor Sardine in his tracks.

"Sit!" he shouted out to the dogs. "Lie down!"

This only made the dogs growl more fiercely, and one darted forward and gave the assistant a good nip on the leg. This was enough for the two men, who turned around and began to run back up the hill, with Professor Sardine shouting over his shoulder, "You haven't seen the last of me! I'll get you for this!"

Rudolf realized that all was now well, and that Max and Maddy had been given a good start, but he could not resist the temptation of running after Professor Sardine and taking a large bite out of his snowsuit. This shut him up! The enraged professor gave a yelp and stumbled off as fast as he could, with a large, and very cold, hole in the seat of his pants.

"We're going to make it," said Max, as they saw the spire of the village church sticking out of the trees below them.

Maddy gave a shout of joy. "Yes," she said. "I can smell the bakery from here. They're baking marzipan cakes. Can you smell it?"

Max could, and the smell meant safety. He reached out to Rudolf, who was running along beside him.

"Thank you, Rudolf," he said. "I think that you and your friends saved my life up there."

Rudolf gave a bark in reply. It had been a pleasure for him to do what he did. He knew that his grandfather—who had once saved two climbers trapped by an avalanche for three days—would be proud of him. And that was enough reward for a dog.

Down in the village, the local policeman listened to the children's breathless account of what had happened.

"I see," he said. "I've been a bit suspicious of what's been going on up there, but I had no idea that it was the bank robbers we've been hearing about. Well done! You've certainly done a very good job!"

While the policeman telephoned Mr. Huffendorf, the children were given a warm and reviving cup of piping hot chocolate, and each dog was given a large bowl of steaming milk.

Half an hour later, Mr. Huffendorf arrived, together with some more senior policemen wearing skis and carrying all sorts of ropes and ice axes. Mr. Huffendorf shook hands solemnly with the two children and listened in astonishment to their account of what had happened. Then they all went up the hill to the marked tree where the money had been buried, and the policemen, assisted by Rudolf and his friends, dug the crate out from underneath the snow.

In the meantime, some of the other policemen went off in search of Professor Sardine and his assistant. They combed the hillside, and then went up to the farmhouse, but they found no sign of the wicked pair. It seemed as if both of them had just vanished into thin air.

But they did find something. Up at the top, pinned to the trunk of a tree just beyond the cable station, they found a hastily scribbled note.

You may think you've
beaten me. But you
haven't! BEWARE!
Professor Claude Sardine
is not so easily vanquished!
So just you BEWARE!

"He's always like that," explained Max. "Nobody ever really catches him. They get close, but he always slips away."

"One day," said Mr. Huffendorf. "One day he'll be caught, and I rather think it'll be you two who do the catching!"

"Perhaps," said Max. "Who knows?"

Back at Mr. Huffendorf's house, a large party had started. Mr. Huffendorf had telephoned all his banker friends to tell them the good news and invite them to come and thank Max and Maddy in person. The money had been counted and returned to the banks, and a telephone call had been put through to Mr. and Mrs. Twist to tell them of the successful outcome of the case.

"I shall always be grateful to you," said Mr. Huffendorf. "Indeed, all Swiss banks will be grateful to you."

At this, all Mr. Huffendorf's banker friends clapped their hands and cheered. This was unusual for the Swiss, who are normally fairly quiet, but it was a very special occasion, after all.

Max and Maddy left Switzerland the next day. But before they left, Mr. Huffendorf invited them into his study to discuss their payment.

"You'll remember that I said you could have it in money or chocolate," he said. "That offer still holds. Which would you prefer?"

Max turned to Maddy, and the two of them had a quick, whispered discussion. Then he turned back and announced their choice.

"Chocolate money," he said. "If that's all right with you."

Mr. Huffendorf clapped his hands with delight. "What a clever choice," he said. "That way you get both. I shall immediately arrange for it to be delivered to you at the station."

They said farewell, and they both gave Rudolf and the other dogs a very special hug.

"These dogs will all be returned to their owners," said Mr. Huffendorf. "All of them, except Rudolf, were the victims of kidnapping by those wicked men. Now their owners will get them back."

Mr. Huffendorf drove them to the station and said good-bye on the platform, and then

the two children boarded the train and set-
tled down in their seats.

"Oh," said Maddy suddenly. "We forgot
about the chocolate money!"

Max smiled. "Look up," he said.

Maddy did. There, above their heads,
neatly stacked on the luggage racks, were ten
large sacks, each of them stuffed full of
delicious-looking chocolate coins.

"That'll keep us going for years!" exclaimed
Maddy. "What a generous present."

Max nodded. "Perhaps we should try just
one or two," he said. "I promise not to eat too
many before we get home."

Max really meant that promise, but there
are some promises that are just too hard to
keep. I'm sure you understand what I mean,
don't you?

A Note on the Author

Alexander McCall Smith has written more than fifty books, including the bestselling No. 1 Ladies' Detective Agency mysteries, the Sunday Philosophy Club series, and many children's stories. A professor of medical law at Edinburgh University, he was born in what is now Zimbabwe and currently lives in Scotland. Visit him at www.alexandermccallsmith.com.

A Note on the Illustrator

Macky Pamintuan has illustrated several chapter books and picture books. Originally from the Philippines, he now lives in California with his wife, Aymone, and their dog, Winter. Visit him at www.mackyart.com.

Don't miss any adventure, mystery, and fun with these

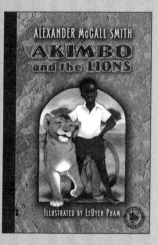

Alexander McCall Smith titles!